Christmas With The Cupcake Boy

MEN OF MELBOURNE, Volume 2

Alex Leslie

Published by Alex Leslie, 2022.

CHRISTMAS WITH THE CUPCAKE BOY

First edition. March 1, 2022.

ISBN: 979-8201330378

Written by Alex Leslie.

Table of Contents

For Rob

Thank you for all your support on this journey. I don't have the words to express how blessed I am to have a friend like you in my life.

So in lieu of words, allow me to express how blessed I am through lots of big hugs and gentle gropes... :)

Chapter 1

ALEX WAS in the master bedroom, packing the last of their bags in readiness for the long awaited Christmas mini-break he had arranged for himself and his loving partner Nick. It was early morning, and the warm December sun was streaming through the big picture window behind their bed, bathing the room in soft, golden light.

Christmas in Australia is far from being a Winter Wonderland. Unlike the Northern Hemisphere, most places south of the equator experience the yuletide season during the height of Summer. No snowmen. No snow. Just heat, humidity and the blazing sun above. It's not uncommon for many Aussie families to visit the beach on Christmas Day, and enjoy fresh seafood and salads rather than a traditional roast turkey. A game of backyard cricket after lunch is the order of the day, followed by a relaxed afternoon with friends and family.

Since neither Alex or Nick had any family to spend the holiday season with, it was the perfect opportunity for the two men to get away from it all for a week and unwind after a stressful year.

While searching online travel sites and search engines for a suitable holiday destination, Alex had found an amazing luxury resort near the Mornington Peninsula called the Paradise Beach Resort and Spa, only a few hours drive from the centre of Melbourne.

Assuming they were blessed with clear traffic, they would arrive at the resort sometime before lunch. Private and secluded, they could both relax, unwind, enjoy hot stone massages, five star cuisine and pampering spa treatments. A wonderful way for Alex and Nick to spend their first Christmas together.

Nick was busy loading everything into the SUV and double checking they had everything they would need for a week away. Alex was thankful he had managed to persuade his partner to agree to this little trip. Nick had been running himself ragged at work lately, and the man was in desperate need of some downtime. The Christmas season was the perfect time to forget about the office, the company and the endless meetings his partner was required to attend as owner and CEO of Hawke's Gym – Australia's most popular chain of fitness centres. Nick's recent plans to expand the business into South East Asia and across the Pacific region had only increased his workload and stress. Alex knew his partner would never admit it, but he desperately needed a break. So Alex had gone out of his way to find the most relaxing, stress-free trip he could arrange.

Nick returned to the bedroom and picked up the last of their bags.

"Is that everything?"

"Not quite" Alex said, walking over to the bed and pulling a hunk of plastic mistletoe from under his pillow. He dangled it over his head and looked at Nick with a sly smile. Nick dropped the bag, stalked over and gave Alex a quick kiss.

"You're a goof."

"I'm your goof"

"Damn right, you are!" Nick said with a playful growl, kissing him again, this time more deeply, then grabbed the mistletoe and stuffed it into the front pocket of the remaining travel bag.

"It might come in handy later" Nick said with a sly smile.

Alex smiled back and marveled at Nick, who was as much of a goof as he was. Nick picked up the last bag and proceeded downstairs to load it into the back of the car. Alex grabbed his walking cane from beside the bed and slowly followed in Nick's wake. After one last check to ensure the house was locked up tight, they were ready to leave Melbourne behind and begin their holiday.

Alex settled in the front passenger seat, knowing full well that Nick, dominant and as Alpha male as they came, would insist on driving. As he put on his seatbelt, Alex marveled at the recently upgraded car seats. The new lumbar supports and built in vibrating massagers made their car trips so much more comfortable for Alex.

Living with a spinal injury is no picnic, and driving (or more often than not, being driven) was just one of those activities Alex had gotten used to being uncomfortable and something to endure. But, when Alex had mentioned his discomfort to Nick in passing, Nick had insisted on upgrading the seats on both of their vehicles. Alex had initially resisted the expensive change, since a travel cushion would have sufficed in the short term, but Nick made a point of researching better seats and took care of it. Nick always took care of everything. That was his special nature. While the cost had been astronomical, Alex had to admit the new seats were worth every penny.

As they pulled out of the driveway and headed out onto the street, Alex connected his phone to the car's sound system and searched for something for them to listen to on their journey. He eventually settled on a comedy podcast they both enjoyed. He settled into his now gently vibrating seat as they began their trip up the coast.

As he looked out the window and watched the city streets flash by, his thoughts turned to how much his life had changed over the last year. This time last year, Alex was living as a virtual recluse in a tiny house in the inner city of Melbourne. He had been hiding out for over seven years, avoiding contact with the outside world as much as possible. Living in fear that his psychopathic stalker of an ex would find him. Jack had left him disabled, scarred and convinced he would spend the rest of his life miserable and alone.

It was only after he met Nick on one of his rare trips into the real world that Alex's life changed for the better. With his violent ex now no longer a threat and the need to hide finally over, Alex had managed to regain his freedom and rejoin the rest of the human race.

Admittedly, moving in with Nick had initially been an adjustment, to say the least. Having lived in total isolation for so many years, it took some time to get used to cohabitation with another person. But Nick was patient, kind and understanding. Alex also found that having someone else around was a refreshing change of pace from the staggering loneliness he was used to, and living with someone who loved and supported him unconditionally was beyond anything he had ever hoped for.

Alex had moved his business, making internet cupcake recipe video and writing cookbooks, from his old home to the CBD office building that Nick owned. CupcakeBoy Inc was now a fully staffed video production business, with dedicated teams of social media managers, video production crew, writing assistants and business support staff. Rather than trying to do everything himself, Alex could now rely of his team to do the heavy lifting, which left him more time to focus on building the business and exploring the world he was now free to be a part of.

To be honest, Nick wasn't the only one in need of a break from work. Alex had spent the last few months working on his new "Healthy Cupcakes" cookbook – a joint project between himself and Nick's business. Progress was slow going, but he'd managed to come up with some surprisingly good recipes that were not only healthy, but didn't taste like a toxic waste dump.

As much as he loved his work, it had been fairly stressful implementing such widespread changes to a business he had been running single-handedly for the best part of a decade. Making those changes in only a few short months had only ratcheted up his stress levels.

So having the opportunity to escape the rat race for a week and unwind in the lap of luxury was just what Alex needed. Getting to spend that time with the man he loved only made the deal sweeter.

He looked over at Nick, and smiled at his man's stern facial expression. Nick always had this look of sharp, hyper-concentrated focus when he was driving. Almost like a race car driver or a soldier driving a tank through hostile territory. Nick drove smoothly, precisely and carefully, and Alex never felt anything but completely safe when his man was behind the wheel.

After a long scenic drive up the coast, which Alex took the opportunity to take many photos of as they passed the astonishingly beautiful coastal vistas, the GPS system directed them off the main highway on to a series of back roads until they reached a quiet, treelined road with no houses or businesses. The further along the road they drove, the quieter it seemed to get. The resort's website wasn't kidding when they said it was private and out of the way.

However, when they approached the end of the road, a literal dead end road, Alex and Nick finally saw signs of civilisation. What appeared to be an old style motel with it's frontage mostly dominated by overgrown bushes and shrubs. A large, poorly maintained neon sign on the roof read 'Paradise Beach Motor Inn'

When they pulled up in front of the old motel, the GPS unit ominously announced they had 'arrived at their final destination.'

Alex gulped.

Chapter 2

NICK LOOKED at the 1960's style motel, which had clearly seen better days and currently looked like it was abandoned, with a deep sense of foreboding. He looked toward Alex with raised eyebrows, and was met with a similar look of puzzlement.

This can't be the right place. The GPS must have screwed up.

Alex opened his satchel bag and pulled out the printed email confirming their reservation. Nick examined the GPS, and checked the entered address against the address on the email. They were identical.

"This can't be right. This doesn't look like a luxury resort" Nick muttered, looking out the window in hopes of seeing something that would explain the situation. But there was nothing.

A thought occurred to him. Maybe this was some kind of hipster thing? Hipsters are always opening wacky businesses filled with old crap and useless junk. Like that stupid cafe Alex had dragged Nick into a few weekends ago. Instead of comfortable chairs, they were forced to sit on old beer kegs and drank coffee out of 'upcycled' baked bean cans. Even Alex, open minded and willing to try almost any new food fad, thought the whole thing was utterly ridiculous. They left quickly and found a proper cafe. One great thing about Melbourne: there's no shortage of cafes.

Nah, hipsters wouldn't run a resort. Even their demented love of irony wouldn't extend to holidaying in a run-down old dump like this.

Nick shook off his flight of fancy, and looked over at Alex. His features were etched with worry, like he was upset.

"Hey, don't worry. We'll find the resort. It's probably just a misprint on the email or something."

Alex nodded, his tense shoulders relaxing slightly, then grabbed his walking stick and stepped out of the car.

"Where are you going?" Nick said with slight alarm.

"To ask for directions. There's a reception office over there," he pointed toward a small office with a glass front entry door with a wooden frame marred by aged flaking paint, "Chances are they'll know where the resort is."

Nick leapt out of the car, locked it with the remote and chased after Alex. He didn't like the look of this place. It gave him the creeps. He certainly didn't like the idea of Alex wandering around such a place. The place is probably filled with squatters or drug addicts. He reached Alex just as he made his way into the small reception office.

Nick grabbed Alex's arm and held him in place. Alex yelped.

"Don't go running off by yourself. I don't like the look of this place."

"It's just an old motel. What's the worst that could happen?"

"Didn't we watch 'Psycho' just last week?"

Alex hadn't ever been a fan of horror movies. Given his history, that's not even remotely surprising. But Nick and Alex's mutual love of old movies had lead them to having a Hitchcock marathon one weekend, and when he saw Psycho was part of the DVD bundle they had bought online, he decided to give it a go. He'd asked Nick if it contained explicit violence or stabbing scenes, and Nick had been upfront and honest about the movie, explaining what Alex could expect without too many spoilers. He reluctantly agreed it was probably okay to watch, so long as Nick held him tight. So they had watched the film together, Alex cuddled up in Nick's lap, and despite a few shrieks during the infamous 'shower scene' Alex had enjoyed the film, and understood why it was widely considered such a masterpiece.

"This isn't the Bates Motel!" Alex scoffed, trying to hide his amusement.

"No, the Bates Motel was the Ritz compared to this place." Nick almost growled.

"You're overreacting. I'll just ring the desk bell and ask for directions. If Norman Bates comes at me in his mother's dress brandishing a knife, you can defend me with your big strong muscles and then tell me 'I told you so' every day until the end of time. Sound fair?"

Nick was not happy about this, but he couldn't help smirking when Alex made mention of his muscles. He knew his boy was being silly, but Nick loved getting his ego stroked. He wouldn't let anything happen to Alex. So he let go of his boy's arm and allowed him to step up to the old, wooden reception desk and ring the bell.

The desk, which was more of a partition that split the room in half, was unremarkable but clean. Behind it was a closed door, which probably led to a back office or perhaps a private staff area. The wall next to the door was dominated with a large, dark stained, wooden pigeon hole shelf. Room keys dangled from hooks below each pigeon hole. There was no computer or modern equipment to speak of. Just an old touchtone desk phone which was covered in a thick layer of dust. It was doubtful the phone had been used much in years.

Nick looked out the windows toward the vacant parking lot. The old pavers that lined the lot were cracked and dotted with weeds. This motel had clearly not been open for a very long time.

We're wasting our time. This place is a ghost town.

"Come on, Alex. There's nobody back there. Let's go back to the car and..."

Suddenly, the door behind the desk opened and a man in his fifties with dark, silver-streaked hair came out, looking surprised. Nick was immediately on his guard.

"Can I help you gentlemen?" the man said cautiously, looking at Alex and then Nick, clearly intimidated by Nick's large size and probably scowling face.

"Yes," Alex said cheerily, apparently putting the man at ease, "We need some help. Would you be able to direct us to the Paradise Beach Resort and Spa, please?"

The man's face was a study of puzzlement. He scratched the back of his neck, like he was trying to think of how to answer.

"Resort? I don't know of any resort around here. I only just moved to the area, but I'm pretty sure there aren't any spas."

Alex visibly deflated, and Nick's heart sank. Alex had been so excited about taking this trip. It was not becoming obvious that there was no resort, and they had fallen victim to an elaborate scam. Nick could tell from his boy's face that Alex had come to the same conclusion.

"I don't understand. This is the correct address, and the website was so professional..."

"Well, as you can see, we aren't even open for business yet. We've only just started stripping the place out before we... wait, did you say website?" the man behind the desk said.

"Yes," Alex handed over the printed email receipt and showed the man the address and logo.

The man shuddered, his features tightened and his eyes closed briefly. When he opened them again, he turned toward the office door behind him and called out "Billy! Billy, get your butt out here this instant!" in a raised voice that sounded part angry, part frustrated.

Nick and Alex looked at each other, hoping the other could offer and explanation for what was going on.

Moments later, a young boy, no older than fifteen or so, came through the door.

"Uncle Bob?"

"You wanna explain this?" Bob thrust the printed email at the teenager, who looked at it and blanched.

"Oh no! This wasn't supposed to happen. The site wasn't supposed to go live yet! I swear, this is all a mistake!"

Nick looked at the kid, who was clearly panicking, and tried to relax his features so he didn't seem so intimidating.

"What wasn't supposed to happen?" Nick asked in a soft, calming tone.

"I wanted to help Uncle Bob by setting up a website and booking portal for the motel. When the renovations are complete and we're open for business, I wanted to surprise him with the website. But it wasn't supposed to be up and online yet. I must have accidentally 'published' the site, instead of setting it to 'private' so only I could access it..." the kid rambled on, he looked like he was on the verge of tears.

"You built a website?" Bob said, "But we haven't even started the renovations! Isn't that jumping the gun a bit?"

"Hang on, so you own this motel?" Alex asked, trying to get everything straight in his head.

"Yeah, I bought it last month for cheap. I figured we could restore it to its former glory. Add all the mod-cons and turn it into luxury holiday accommodation. Retro but civilised. Attract the hipster dollar."

"Hipsters! I knew it was hipsters!" Nick said with a combination of accusation and vindication. Alex looked at him with raised eyebrows, as if he had suddenly grown a second head.

"So, we've come all this way for nothing. No hot stone massages? No spa treatments? No five star cuisine?" Alex said with dejected bitterness.

"Spa treatments?! What the hell did you put on that website, Billy?" Bob said with puzzlement.

"I just wanted to make the place sound amazing. Maybe I got a little carried away."

"This is illegal, Billy!" Bob waved the email receipt in the teenager's face, "This is blatant false advertising. This could get us shut down before we even open. They could sue us for this!" he turned to Alex, "Please, please don't sue us. I swear I had no idea about the website."

Nick had heard enough. He stepped forward and took charge of the situation.

"Okay, first things first. Alex, you paid a deposit, right?"

Alex nodded sheepishly.

"I want the deposit refunded right now. Next, I want that website shut down immediately, before anyone else sees it and wastes their time coming here."

Billy reached under the reception desk and pulled out a laptop. He opened it and started typing furiously. Bob stood next to him looking pale. Nick believed the poor man genuinely had no idea what was going on.

"It's done. The website is offline and can't be accessed by anyone. The refund is being sent through now. It should show up in your bank account by the end of the day. I'm really, really sorry. I didn't mean any of this to happen. Are you..." the teenager gulped, "Are you gonna call the police?"

Bob looked panicked.

"No." Alex said with finality.

What? Are you insane?

"Alex, perhaps we should discuss this in private for a moment?"

"This was an honest mistake. He didn't mean for this to happen. Alright, it's a pain in the ass and I'm disappointing that our holiday is ruined, but I don't believe there was any malice behind it. He was just trying to do something nice for his uncle, and got a little carried away."

Nick scowled at Alex. He hated it when his boy was so calm and logical.

"Fine, no police." Nick turned his attention to Billy, "But this better not happen again. I'm going to be keeping a close eye on you. Any more dodgy websites and I'll be calling our Detective friend in Melbourne and see what he thinks about it, clear?"

I'll have my security guy monitor Billy's IP address and make sure this doesn't happen again.

"I swear, it won't happen again. I promise"

Nick nodded at the kid and turned back to Alex.

"Alright, let's head back to the car. It's still early. We can make it back home by mid afternoon if the traffic remains light."

Alex's wan smile and sheepish nod damn near broke Nick's heart. One look at his face and it was clear that Alex was blaming himself for this whole disaster. His boy quietly slipped out of the reception office and headed toward the SUV.

"Thank you, sir!" Bob said with relief, "I'm so sorry about all of this. Billy's a good kid, he just gets a bit carried away with that damn computer of his. I promise I'll keep him out of trouble." Bob turned to the teenager, "Billy, how about you go down to the first cabin and start stripping the wallpaper. I'll join you in a minute."

Billy nodded and headed out the door without another word.

"Ever since his parents kicked him out and I took him in, he's been good as gold. Never had an ounce of worry from him. When I bought the motel, I thought it would be a great way for the two of us to work together on something special. Build something for his future. I swear, he didn't mean to do anything wrong..."

"I know," Nick said sighed, "He seems like a good kid. Why did they kick him out?"

Bob shifted uncomfortably, "They found out he was gay and decided they'd rather he didn't live with them anymore. He's fifteen years old, for crying out loud! How could they do that?"

Nick nodded sympathetically. Billy reminded him of himself. Nick too, had left home at an early age after coming out and being rejected by his parents. Coincidentally, like Billy, Nick had also been taken in by his uncle. Bob seemed like a good, solid man who would look after Billy and give him the love and care he needed.

Nick reached into his pocket and pulled out his wallet. He removed one of the crisp, white business cards he always carried and handed it to Bob.

"Keep encouraging his computer skills, he's got real talent. If he could build a site that detailed, he could have a big future ahead of him in web design. When he graduates high school, tell him to give me a call. I might be able to get him into a traineeship."

"Wow, thanks Mr..." Bob looks at the business card, "Hawke? As in Hawke's Gym? I thought I recognised you. I promise to keep encouraging him. He's a good kid, and I only want the best for him."

Nick nodded and stalked out of the office. When he got back to the SUV, Alex was sitting there looking like a kicked puppy.

"I'm sorry about all this. I can't believe I fell for a fake website..."

"Hey!" Nick cut him off mid-sentence, "You aren't to blame here. You showed me that site after you made the booking, and I didn't see anything untoward either. That kid is a web design genius. Hopefully this experience will make him a little more responsible, so he can use his powers for good from now on."

Alex smiled slightly, his face brightening as Nick lightened the mood.

"But what about our holiday? What are we going to do now? It's too late to book anything."

"As long as I'm with you, I don't care if we go on holiday. We can just hang around the house. We'll go on a proper holiday another time. It's not a big deal."

"Really? You're not disappointed?"

"Well, it would have been nice to have those couple's massages, but I don't care about that stuff. As long as we have each other, what more could I possibly need?"

Alex smiled wide, his eyes shimmered with unshed tears, and Nick leaned forward and kissed his boy deeply, taking each other's breath away.

Nick reached over and put Alex's seatbelt on, then bucked himself in as he started the car. He pulled the car out of the motel's driveway and head back down the road that brought them there, heading toward the highway.

Chapter 3

ALEX WAS absolutely mortified. Their first ever Christmas together and the whole thing had turned into a complete and utter disaster. He couldn't believe he hadn't thought to more thoroughly check out the details of the 'resort' before they drove all the way out there. A simple phone call could have avoided this entire mess.

Above all else, Alex was most upset for Nick. The whole point of this little getaway was to help his lover relax and unwind after months of stress at work. Now, just days before Christmas, it was far too late in the game to book anything else. They were stuck in Melbourne for the holidays.

"This isn't your fault, babe, so stop brooding."

"I'm still sorry. I just can't believe this happened. I was just so looking forward to us having a nice, relaxing and quiet Christmas together."

"Like I said, It's not your fault. That kid made an amazing website. You should hire him next time you want to refresh yours."

Alex knew Nick was trying to lighten the mood, but it was still a kick in the head to have been so completely taken in by a fifteen year old with a laptop, regardless of it all being an innocent mistake. Considering he had built an entire career around online content and being internet-savvy. He felt like an imbecile.

Alex tried to shake his cloudy mood. It was only just passed midday, and they would be back in the city in a couple of hours. Once they got home, he would have to find a way to make it all up to Nick.

A few minutes later, Nick pulled the car over at a small, beachside seafood restaurant and the two men got out to stretch their legs and have a nice, leisurely lunch together. They shared a huge 'Fisherman's Basket' platter loaded with fresh oysters, king prawns, scallops, crispy friend fish cocktails, locally caught crab and more hot chips than two people could ever hope to consume. Nick hand fed the oysters to Alex, something Alex had never tried before, and his mood brightened significantly. He savoured the light, briny flavour and the sharpness of the fresh lemon juice that Nick squeezed over each morsel.

In the end they couldn't possibly finish the entire platter, which Alex suspected was actually designed to feed a party of six, and the waitress kindly packed up their leftovers into two large boxes to take home with them. They returned to the car, found something lighthearted to listen to for the return journey, and headed back out onto the road.

By the time they got home, Alex felt better about the situation, but was aching all over. Long car trips were a killer on his back, and he obviously hadn't expected to do the return trip to Melbourne on the same day. Alex was stiff as a board and his muscles spasmed as he slowly made his way out to the kitchen to make coffee. By the time he had finished wrangling the devil machine into making two steaming mugs of Mocha Supreme, Nick had taken their bags back upstairs and unpacked everything.

They sat at the kitchen table, sipped their coffees and Nick picked at the leftovers from lunch. Alex stared in wonder as his man demolished what was essentially a second lunch. Nick's appetite was nothing short of insatiable. I guess when you're a muscle-bound god who spends half his life in the gym, you need all the calories you can get. Even still, Alex couldn't help wondering where Nick put it all. It would forever be an irony that while Alex was the chubby one, he ate like a bird compared to his lover.

When the coffees were finished and the leftovers but a distant memory, Nick suggested they go out onto the entertainment deck and enjoy a long, hot soak in the outdoor jacuzzi.

"That sounds like a wonderful idea. My back could use it. I'll go set it up, you go grab the robes and towels."

Nick smiled and headed off to the downstairs bathroom to collect the supplies. Alex had bought the jacuzzi a few months after moving in with Nick, as he had missed having regular spa baths since leaving his old house. Nick had suggested remodeling the master bathroom upstairs and putting the spa in there, but Alex liked the idea of having an outdoor bath. The deck was large and secluded, plus the view of the garden was magnificent.

By the time Nick returned with the towels, robes and two bottles of water, Alex had the hot tub bubbling away and ready to use. They slipped into the warm water and let the jets melt away any residual tension. They watched the sun slowly set, turning the sky a beautiful bright orange, then pink, and eventually a dark swirling opal as the first stars began twinkling above them. While it wasn't quite how Alex had expected their day to end, he couldn't deny the majestic night sky was nothing short of breathtaking.

-

The next morning, the two men were enjoying a light breakfast of fruit salad and toast when Nick's phone began ringing.

"Sorry, babe. It's Lara." Nick said softly.

Nick answered the call from his assistant, and almost immediately, Alex could see the waves of tension rolling off of him.

Why is Lara calling? He's supposed to be on holidays!

"What do you mean they just showed up? What the hell are they doing here?" Nick almost shouted. He was scowling, and Alex knew from experience that something had not gone to plan. Nick didn't like the unexpected, especially at work.

"But they aren't supposed to meet with us until next month, Lara. We aren't ready to do the pitch yet. How the hell did this happen?"

Alex cleared away the breakfast plates. He knew where this was going. Within minutes, Nick would be driving into the office to stop the sky from falling. Alex would bet money on it.

"Well, stall them. Make them coffee. Offer them breakfast. Do whatever you have to do! I'm leaving now, I'll be in the office as soon as possible."

BINGO! We have a winner!

Nick ended the call and growled as he stalked around the kitchen looking for his keys.

"In the fruit bowl next to the coffee machine." Alex answered Nick's unspoken question. Nick snagged the keys and quickly kissed Alex on the cheek.

"Sorry, babe. I have to run. Remember those big investors from Malaysia who I'm due to meet next month? Well, apparently someone at their office got their wires crossed and they've shown up for the meeting in December instead of January. All hell is breaking loose. I have to get over to the office before they walk out and the deal goes bust."

Alex sighed and nodded, "No worries, get out of here. Give Lara my best and I'll see you when I see you."

"I love you, Alex."

"I love you too, gorgeous,. Now, go, Before you get caught in traffic."

Nick kissed him again, then dashed across the kitchen, through to the garage and was into the car and gone within moments.

Alex could have gone with him to the office. He was sure he could find something in his own office to occupy his time, but they were supposed to be on holiday. Alex didn't want to fill his day with shuffling papers and pointless busy work. He wanted to relax, and he wanted Nick to relax too. This expansion deal was going to be the death of him. Nick wasn't used to this much stress, and it wasn't healthy. Alex had to do something about it.

Alex pulled out his phone. He needed to text Lara. While they aren't exactly friends, they've had lunch together several times. He also had an ace up his sleeve if he needed it.

Alex: *After today, Nick is officially on holiday. You need to make sure he isn't disturbed any further. No more calls unless it's an emergency.*

Lara: *I love you, honey. But you do realise I'm not YOUR assistant, right?*

Alex: *I'm serious, Lara. He really needs a break. Unless the building is on fire, no more calls after today.*

Lara: *I can't promise that. You know I can't.*

Alex: *Then I can't promise Nick won't find out who ate all the chocolate protein bars from the secret stash in his office...*

Lara: *You wouldn't!*

Alex: *They're his favourite, Lara. What kind of horrible, selfish person would steal their boss's favourite treats?*

Lara: *This is really low...*

Alex: *I can't imagine how he'll react when he finds out...*

Lara: *FINE! No more calls. But you are a bad person and pure evil.*

Alex: *Merry Christmas to you too :)*

Lara: *Lunch next week?*

Alex: *Sure. Text me ;)*

Once the breakfast dishes were washed, dried and put away, he went out to the lounge room and pulled out his laptop. After a quick search of various last-minute travel sites, it was confirmed that there was absolutely no possibility of booking another trip until well after the new year. So much for trying to find another spa resort.

Then Alex had an idea. A brilliant idea. They were going to have a luxury resort holiday after all. But he would need some help to make it happen. Alex pulled out his phone and called his assistant. Kelly answered within one ring.

"Alex? Aren't you supposed to be getting wrapped in seaweed and beaten to pulp by a hot Swedish guy?"

"What the hell kind of resort did you think I was going to?"

"I dunno, I've never been to one before. What's happening?"

Alex recounted the details of their disastrous trip to the Paradise Beach Motor Inn. Kelly was silent for a moment, then burst out laughing.

"It's not funny! It's a nightmare!"

"I'm sorry. I blame my heartlessness on being stuck here doing paperwork in a near empty office."

"Well, consider yourself reassigned. I need your help and we don't have much time. Get over to my place now. We've got shopping to do!"

At the mention of 'shopping' Kelly squealed with excitement, then hung up.

Alex grabbed his laptop and started furiously typing, looking for everything he would need to buy, borrow and steal to make his idea happen.

Chapter 4

NICK WAS absolutely furious as he drove in to the office. He couldn't believe the massive deal he had spent more than six months working on was hanging in the balance because someone couldn't read a fucking calendar correctly.

Nick had been in negotiations with representatives from Bityang Corp. in Malaysia to help fund the upcoming expansion into South East Asia. Having local investors on the ground made good business sense, as they could help oversee construction and anticipate local issues that may need to be addressed. But the final meeting and contract signing was supposed to be held at the end of January, not today. Apparently, someone had misprinted something somewhere, and the representatives had arrived in Australia a whole month early. It's not like Nick could tell them "Sorry, you showed up a month early. Come back later…" without jeapordising the deal. So here he was, driving like a NASCAR driver, desperate to reach the office before his investors got frustrated and left.

He made it into the building in record time, and quickly dashed into his private office to change into the spare business shirt and dress trousers he always kept there. Lara, his insanely efficient personal assistant, had already taken them out of the cupboard and even polished his dress shoes to save him time.

Lara is amazing. I need to give her a raise.

Once changed, Nick met Lara outside his office. Her expression was tight, but appeared to be calm.

"I put them in the conference room, gave them coffee and set them up with a special 'Australian Breakfast' delivered from the cafe downstairs. When they asked where you were, I told them it was an Australian tradition to give our guests food and drink before meeting with them. I don't think they believed me, but they were very excited to try the Egg and Bacon Rolls and Raisin Toast."

Nick smirked. Lara was the queen of thinking on her feet. He doubted there was a single situation that she could n't talk her way out of.

I should put her in the sales department. We'd own half the world by lunchtime!

"I want you to go through every single piece of correspondence we've had with Bityang Corp. Letters, memos, emails, smoke signals, telepathic visions – everything. I want to know if it was their screw up or ours. If it was theirs, so be it. If it was ours, find out who is responsible. Heads are going to roll if we lose this deal."

Lara blanched momentarily, but quickly recovered, nodded sharply and immediately went to her desk and began going through everything. Nick squared his shoulders, took a deep breath, put a welcoming smile on his face and headed into the conference room.

-

The meeting dragged on forever. The investors had loved their 'traditional' Aussie breakfast and after a few hours, they asked to be taken out for lunch so they could experience more 'traditional' Australian foods. Nick suspected they we're very much aware that Lara's creative stalling had been a thin tissue of lies, but they clearly didn't mind – especially when Nick took them to out to an expensive restaurant over on Lygon Street. Nick made no attempt to claim the obviously Italian dishes the restaurant served were in any way Australian, but the investors didn't care when the wine started flowing.

By the time the meeting was concluded, the contracts signed, and hands were shaken, the day was well and truly over. The sun had set and Nick had only one thing on his mind – Alex.

Alex had taken yesterday's events to heart and Nick hated that his boy blamed himself for something that was completely out of his control. Nick resolved to take Alex's mind off the whole resort fiasco with one of his patented distraction techniques as soon as he got home.

As Nick got into the car, he considered stopping off somewhere and grabbing dinner for them both. But it was already past dinner time, and Alex may have already cooked something. Better check in with his boy and find out what's happening at home.

Oh, damn! My phone battery is dead. I forgot to charge it last night.

Nick reached for the phone charger he always kept in the car, but suddenly remembered it was still in Alex's car. He'd neglected to take it out when they got back from the Bates Motel.

Bugger! I'll just go home and play it by ear. I can always pick something up later if worst comes to worst.

Nick started the engine, pulled out of the underground car park beneath his building, and headed out into the evening traffic. Traffic was reasonably light, given that peak hour was well and truly over. The drive home should be quick.

When Nick finally made it home, he parked in the driveway rather than in the garage. If he needed to head out again to pick up dinner or something, it would save time. As he walked up to the front door, Nick noticed something sitting on the welcome mat. A large bulky blob. In the dark, it was difficult to see what it was. He reached down carefully, and touched it lightly. Something hard and spiky.

A pineapple! Why is there a pineapple on my door mat?

Nick picked up the pineapple, which oddly had a piece of red Christmas tinsel wrapped around the neck, and fumbled for his keys to unlock the door.

Once inside, Nick froze on the spot. He looked around the room and didn't know what was going on.

Am I in the wrong house? What's happened to my living room?

The usually cold, stark, art gallery-like living room had been completely transformed. The room had been filled with at least a dozen large potted palm trees, each decorated with tinsel, twinkle lights and Christmas ornaments. An enormous yellow surfboard was propped up against the back of the couch. The walls had been decorated with colourful flower garlands, which appeared to be made of paper. The rest of the room was filled with palm fronds and cardboard cut-out tiki statues. But most bizarre of all, on every available surface, from the coffee table to the mantelpiece, was a truly staggering number of pineapples. Some decorated with tinsel. Others were wearing sunglasses. The rest were just plain pineapples, lounging around the living room.

What the hell is going on?

There was no sign of Alex anywhere. Although with all the palm trees are pineapples, he could be standing a foot away and Nick wouldn't see him.

"Alex? Alex are you here?"

"Aloha!" Alex's disembodied voice came from somewhere toward the kitchen. When Nick headed over there, he was stopped in his tracks by Alex, who emerged from the kitchen dressed in a garish hot pink Hawaiian shirt, which he wore open to the waist. The shirt was decorated with surfboards and pineapples. Alex's unexpected costume was accented by a grass skirt, which Nick suspected was made of plastic, and an equally plastic lei around his neck.

Alex smiled broadly, walked over to Nick and placed a lei over his head and kissed him gently on the cheek.

"Welcome to Hawaii, Sir!"

"Um, thanks. Whats going on?"

"Isn't it obvious?"

"Not exactly…"

Alex giggled and motioned for Nick to come and sit down on the couch.

"You see, since our trip to the resort turned out to be a complete bust, I decided to create a little resort of our own, so we can relax and enjoy ourselves, all from the comfort of our own home. Plus, no travelling required!" Alex explained.

"And, all this?" Nick gestured around at the room.

"Well, I thought a tropical resort seemed like a fun idea, and the 'Hawaiian' theme was a lot easier to put together than if I'd gone with a 'Bali' theme instead. Those giant concrete Buddha statues were way too heavy and so expensive."

Nick was totally lost, but loved Alex's enthusiasm for whatever the hell this was. Alex quickly went back to the kitchen and returned moments later with cocktails. The drinks were, of course, Hawaiian themed and served out of hollowed out pineapples with twisty straws and little paper umbrellas.

Alex handed him one of the pineapple concoctions and Nick couldn't contain his laughter any longer. The whole thing was completely over-the-top, deranged and wonderful. No one had ever made him a tropical resort before.

"You are completely insane, you know that, right?"

"Yeah, but you love it, don't ya?" Alex said with a cheeky grin.

"Yeah, I do."

The two men clinked their pineapples together, and took long sips of the refreshing cocktail, while appeared to be pineapple juice, white rum and a splash of Midori.

"Our Christmas holiday begins. Cheers!"

Chapter 5

DESPITE ONLY having had a day to organise and set everything up, Alex was very happy with his efforts to transform their home into a Hawaiian-themed holiday resort and spa. He was genuinely amazed at how much stuff he was able to find online using just search engines and social media.

Finding the local party supplies store that was closing down was a stroke of luck too. The guy on Facebook with a garage full of pool party stuff left over from his Luau-themed birthday party a few months ago? That was nothing short of a miracle. Everything else was found utilising Kelly's exceptional shopping skills and more than a little savvy negotiating from them both.

Although, Kelly quickly realised her shopping skills were ultimately just a fringe benefit, and the real reason Alex had roped her into helping out was because of her borderline mutant upper body strength. Due to his spinal injury, Alex was strictly forbidden from engaging in any kind of heavy lifting. Not that Kelly minded that much. As an amateur body builder, she relished any opportunity to show off her strength. Plus, a day playing hooky from the office wasn't something she was likely to object to too strongly.

Okay, so most of the food was not authentically Hawaiian, but you would be surprised how 'authentically Hawaiian' any dish can look if you decorate it with enough pineapples and little paper umbrellas. And a lack of pineapples was definitely not a problem.

"Where did all the pineapples come from?" Nick asked while he sipped on his tropical punch, as if picking up on Alex's internal musings.

"I got them cheap from the markets. The guy wanted to get rid of them because the markets are closing over the holidays and he didn't want them all to go to waste."

"But, there's so many of them. What on earth are we going to do with them all?"

"They can be chopped up, frozen and kept for another day. They'll be great for baking, making smoothies, fruit salads..."

Nick didn't look at all convinced. Alex suspected he was going to have to be a lot more creative in selling the pineapple thing, and desperately tried to come up with something convincing on the fly. Then he remembered something and immediately started blushing at the thought.

"...Oh! Um, and I always wanted to test out that thing." Alex said, trying to appear casual, but blushing even more.

"What thing?" Nick grinned, no doubt intrigued by Alex's flushed cheeks.

"Well, you know that thing... about pineapple juice. About it... you know..." Alex felt like his face was on fire. Considering how much sex the two of them had had over the last year, you would think he wouldn't get so embarrassed talking about it.

Nick flashed a wolfish smile, immediately understanding what Alex was talking about, and stalked over to him as a predator stalks it's prey.

"Ohhh, that thing..." he said, his voice low and husky, "I think we should definitely test that out. I could help you gather some conclusive evidence." Nick couldn't be more cocky.

Yeah, but his cockiness is so damn hot!

Nick grabbed a hold of Alex and brushed his lips against that spot on his neck that made Alex's eyes roll into the back of his head. His man was a master of working hot spots, and as Nick's teeth grazed against the sensitive skin, Alex tried to stifle his whimper.

"Hold your horses! Before we get too carried away. You need to go upstairs and change. I've laid out appropriate attire for you on our bed. Get changed and meet me back here, and I'll show you some more of the resort."

Nick looked a little unhappy getting cock-blocked for a costume change, but Alex knew he would love what was coming up next. Plus, Nick was constantly telling him that 'anticipation was half the fun' and it was good to turn the tables on him once in a while. He gave his man a quick, chaste kiss on the cheek, then gave him a gentle swat on the backside to get him moving. Nick smiled, and headed up the stairs toward their bedroom.

Alex removed the silly grass skirt, which was visually acceptable but had started to make his skin slightly itchy, leaving him wearing just the Hawaiian shirt and the super tight, super skimpy swimming trunks that Nick had insisted on buying him a few weeks ago, in readiness for their trip. Nick had made no secret of the fact that he wanted to see Alex wearing the revealing cozzy as often as possible. Alex, wasn't so sure about wearing them in public, but was happy to indulge his partner in the privacy of their home.

Alex looked out of the kitchen window to the entertainment deck and pool area. He wanted to make sure he hadn't forgotten anything, but everything looked perfect. Well, as perfect as they could be with so little prep time. Moments later, Nick descended the staircase wearing his bright red Hawaiian shirt, buttons undone to reveal his magnificently muscular body; a plastic lei; and of course the equally revealing swimming trunks that Alex had secretly ordered online for his man. The very short shorts were skin tight and framed his bulge obscenely, the sight of which made Alex's mouth went go dry. Nick stalked towards him slowly as their eyes locked, slyly grinning and waggling his eyebrows as Alex enjoyed the stunning view.

"I'm starting to like this resort." Nick said with a playful growl as he caught Alex in his arms and returned to nibbling on his neck. He melted into his arms, moaning with pleasure as Nick once again found that sensitive spot and started working it with his teeth.

"I love you, my Big Kahuna!" Alex said breathlessly, but with more than a little giggle to his voice.

Nick couldn't hold back his chuckle, and brought their lips together, plundering Alex's mouth with his hot tongue.

"Shall we take this upstairs, boy?"

"Not yet, we're going to be late. We're expected at the 'Welcome to Hawaii' Pool Party right now. We don't want to keep the other guests waiting."

"You invited guests?" Nick looked confused. Alex smiled, grabbed his man's hand and led him to the back sliding door.

"Close your eyes. I have a surprise for you."

Nick still looked a little confused, but obediently closed his eyes and allowed himself to be carefully led outside onto the entertainment deck.

"Okay, you can open them now."

When Nick opened his eyes, he took in the scene surrounding him and his face erupted into a joyous smile. The entertainment deck had been completely transformed into what was probably the most eclectic Hawaiian-themed pool party in history.

Strings of twinkle lights had been hung everywhere creating a swirling canopy of multi-coloured brightness. More potted palms gave the wooden structure a more tropical look. The resort 'guests' were a variety of full-sized standing cardboard cut-outs from the closing down party shop, all characters from a recent Star Wars movie, carefully adorned with Hawaiian shirts and leis. The tropical, yet intergalactic, party guests were mingling around the outdoor dining table, as if helping themselves to imaginary drinks canapes. The vision of Luke Skywalker, dressed in a garish Hawaiian shirt and helping himself to a pineapple cocktail, was surreal to say the least. But somehow, it just worked.

And of course, there were more pineapples scattered around every available surface. Okay, even Alex was starting to think he'd gone overboard with the pineapples, but when the market guy had named his price, Alex couldn't resist such a bargain. He was sure they would both be sick of pineapple before New Year, but they would figure out a way to use up the surplus tropical fruit.

"This is absolutely amazing, Alex! I can't believe you did all this in just a day. You are incredible." Nick pulled Alex into a big bear hug, then kissed him tenderly, that joyous smile never leaving his lips.

"Allow me to escort you to our private lagoon, Sir." Alex said with his exaggerated customer service voice. Nick continued to smile and dutifully followed Alex as he walked them toward the pool.

The fenced-in pool area was Alex's crowning glory. More twinkle lights had been threaded through the bars of the pool fence and a few more potted palm trees to give the pool a more lagoon-like quality. Solar powered Tiki torches bathed the whole area in warm, welcoming glow.

Until today, Alex had no idea you could actually rent plants, and he was so thankful when the delivery men had happily unloaded and placed all the palms exactly where he needed them. They would all be collected shortly after Christmas, which was excellent, because Alex couldn't imagine what he would do with thirty potted palm trees if he were stuck with them permanently.

But his greatest find, and by far the bulkiest and most cumbersome decoration, was the six foot high wooden Tiki statue that now stood proudly at one end of the pool. Facebook guy had been so relieved to have Alex take it off his hands, as the massive idol weighed over one hundred kilograms and took up way too much of his garage. He had given it to him for free, and Alex wasn't going to say no to that price. In the end, it required an extra trip to transport the idol, along with a lot of elbow grease from Kelly and Facebook guy, but the effect was astonishing. Standing by the pool, you could really believe you were in Hawaii.

"I'm absolutely lost for words. This place looks stunning. Thank you for doing this. I love you so much."

"I love you too. Merry Christmas." Alex gave his man a swift kiss, then carefully stripped off his pink Hawaiian shirt.

"It's been so hot and humid today, I think a dip in the lagoon is in order." Alex smiled, hooked his walking cane onto the grip mount he installed on the pool stairs, then carefully stepped into the cool water.

Nick followed suit, tossing his shirt and following him into the pool. He stalked through the water, fixing Alex with a smouldering stare, and slowly backed Alex against the side of the pool. Nick leaned forward and claimed his lips in a searing, powerful kiss that was equal parts passionate and possessive. Nick moved his hands over Alex's body, feeling, exploring, and eventually settling on his pebbled nipples. He teased and pinched them, making Alex moan and writhe.

"But Sir, what will the other guests think?" Alex said teasingly.

"They'll think they have a great view!" Nick growled, playfully biting Alex's shoulder in that spot that sent a spike of electricity straight to his cock.

"Please don't tell my boss. He'll fire me for fraternising with a guest!" Alex said breathlessly.

"Well, I own this resort, so I guess that makes me your boss's boss. So your service better be exemplary!" Nick said with a wolfish grin.

"Yes, Sir!" Alex giggled, enjoying this little game. He ran his hands down Nick's chiseled torso until he reached his man's swim shorts. He gently squeezed Nick's hardening bulge, and shuddered at Nick's appreciative growl.

Chapter 6

NICK COULDN'T remember a time where he was this turned on before. Alex's decorations, while utterly insane, had certainly set the mood, and the idea of spending a few days alone with his boy in their make-believe tropical paradise was very appealing indeed.

Alex's little role playing game was also very intriguing. The scenario of Nick being the hotel owner and Alex being the employee, his boy being there to do his bidding, was sexy as fuck. It played into all those Dominant/submissive roles the two men had enjoyed since they first got together. In that moment, Nick couldn't understand how they had never tried this kind of role playing before.

Alex's hands gently grasped at the front of Nick's swim shorts, and within moments, Nick could feel his control slipping away.

"You're here to ensure my stay is as *pleasurable* as possible, right?" he growled in his boy's ear, feeling Alex shiver against him.

"Yes, Sir. Anything you need."

"Good."

Nick placed his hands on Alex's shoulders and roughly turned him away to face the wall of the pool.

"Hold onto the wall with both hands. Don't move. I hope you aren't attached to these."

With that, Nick pressed his thumbs into the back of Alex's skimpy swim shorts, tearing the thin fabric and ripping open the back of the garment, revealing his boy's round, plump ass. Alex gasped in mock scandal, but Nick could see Alex was trying to hide the smile on his face.

"I knew you were going to do that," Alex whispered, stifling a giggle, "Lucky you bought me more than one pair..."

Nick silenced him by pushing a finger between his exposed cheeks and pressing against his puckered hole.

"Quiet. You wouldn't want your boss to see you like this. Fraternising with a guest, for shame! So stay quiet, or he'll here you. He's watching right now, but he can't see what I'm doing to you. You better be quiet, or he'll come over here and fire you."

Alex quietly moaned as Nick breached his opening, pressing his finger in gently, moving slowly and rhythmically. Nick's other hand moved slowly up his boy's body to his chest, where he sought out his nipple and began teasing and torturing the little nub. When Nick suddenly grazed that special spot deep inside, Alex couldn't contain the moan that escaped from him. Nick immediately withdrew his finger and shushed his boy.

"I said quiet, boy. If you can't be quiet, I may just have to do something to keep you quiet."

Nick was really enjoying this game. Alex was clearly enjoying it too, if his rapid breathing and flushed face were any indication. Nick didn't expect his boy to remain quiet. Mainly because he had every intention of doing whatever it took to make him squirm and moan and scream out with pleasure. Nick chuckled to himself as he breached Alex's hole again, this time with two fingers. Alex shuddered against him, and Nick could tell he was desperately trying to remain quiet. Nick would have to try a little harder.

Alex is really trying to hold it together, but I really want to shatter his self-control.

Nick quickly pulled down his own swim shorts. The tight material and his achingly hard cock was not a good combination. He'd like nothing more than to fuck Alex senseless in the pool, but without lube it would be painful and awkward for both of them. No matter, they could fuck later. For now, Nick would concentrate on blowing his boy's mind.

Nick continued to tease his boy's nipples while he crooked his fingers and grazed Alex's gland again. He grinned evilly as his boy tried and failed to maintain his composure, gasping out each time Nick touched his internal hot spot.

"Sounds like you need a little help to keep quiet..."

Nick pressed his wide, muscular chest against Alex's back. He stopped working on his boy's nipple, instead moving that hand up to cover Alex's mouth, making sure he could still breathe. Nick wasn't into dangerous kinks like breath control.

Nick withdrew his fingers again, reached around and grasped Alex's cock, pumping his hard shaft mercilessly. Nick lined his own cock up with his boy's crease and began thrusting between those round, juicy ass cheeks. He could feel Alex was close, his whole body vibrating as his orgasm began to build. Alex's muffled groan against Nick's fingers was the sexiest sound he had ever heard. He began thrusting harder, growling against his boy's ear as his pumping and thrusting synchronised. As they approached the edge together, both men breathing raggedly, Nick placed his mouth over Alex's shoulder, waited until they were both at the point of no return, then bit down sharply. Alex screamed with pleasure, Nick's hand muffling the sound as both men found their release. He released Alex and both men gasped for air, utterly spent from their sexy little game.

Alex had a massive smile on his face, which Nick couldn't help but return with his own.

"Wow! That was just... wow!" Alex said, "We've never done anything like that before. That was so hot!"

Nick's smile turned wolfish, "We could do something like that again sometime, if you'd like?" to which Alex nodded enthusiastically, the broad smile never leaving his face.

"Come on, let's go wash up, then we can have some dinner." Alex said as he slowly headed toward the stairs and carefully made his way out of the pool. He bashfully covered the huge rip in the back of his swim shorts when he noticed Nick openly admiring his exposed rear.

"Gee, I hope my boss doesn't see me with my uniform in such a state." Alex said with a giggle.

"I have no doubt he would approve," Nick said with a predatory smile, "He may even insist on it becoming a permanent alteration..."

"In your dreams!" Alex laughed.

I'm living my dreams. And all because of you.

Chapter 7

WHILE ALEX had managed a remarkable Hawaiian-themed transformation on the house in a relatively short amount of time, he hadn't really managed to do the same with the kitchen. Alex had simply run out of time to plan out and prepare a suitably Hawaiian-themed dinner menu, with the exception of the tropical cocktails and a staggering abundance of pineapples.

But considering Alex had somehow pulled all of this off from scratch in just a few short hours, he didn't mind having grilled chicken and mixed leaf salad for dinner. He was tempted to garnish their plates with diced pineapple, but thought that was probably going a bit too far. Besides, their simple meal was quick and easy to prepare, and it would leave them more time to enjoy 'Hawaii' if they weren't spending all their time making a more elaborate, more traditional dish. Digging a hole in the backyard and cooking a pig in a buried hot coal pit was a bit more time consuming than Alex was willing to attempt!

"This doesn't seem very Hawaiian." Nick cheekily remarked as he devoured his dinner.

Alex rolled his eyes and smirked, then leaned over the kitchen table and stuck one of the little paper umbrellas into Nick's chicken. Nick snickered.

"We could have just ordered something in, ya know. Save you from cooking after doing all of this."

"I considered that, but I didn't want to break the spell. Besides, you might be surprised to learn their aren't many traditional Hawaiian restaurants that deliver in Melbourne."

Nick mock indignant look of shock and dramatic pouting had Alex in hysterics, which made Nick quickly lose his composure too, leaving him chuckling as he returned his attention to his plate.

"Can I ask you something? This isn't the first time you've done this, is it?"

Alex froze, "What do you mean?"

"All this..." Nick gestured at the decorations around them.

"It's the first time I've done it on such short notice."

"So you have done it before."

"Well, yeah. I lived in that house by myself for seven years. It wasn't like I had the option to go on holiday. So, when I felt the need for a little break from my everyday routine, I'd order in everything I'd need to make my home into the ultimate holiday destination. One year, I 'went' to Japan. England another. I even did a trip down the Amazon River once. The canoe was a bastard to get into the living room, but it was an amazing experience. And all I needed was a little imagination and some online shopping."

Nick's expression was unreadable. Alex wasn't sure what to say, and it seemed Nick didn't know what to say either. Alex suddenly felt a little uncomfortable.

"You probably think it's silly." Alex whispered as he blushed with embarrassment at his own obvious lunacy.

"I think it's amazing."

Alex looked at Nick with skepticism.

"Seriously. I would never have thought of doing something like this. And it's a hell of a lot better than a boring old Christmas tree and some tinsel. I reckon we should do this every Christmas."

"Do you mean it? You really like it? It's not crazy?"

"Oh, it's totally insane, but that's why I love it!" Nick said with a cheeky grin, "This is creative, spontaneous and absolutely brilliant. I can't wait to see what else Hawaii has in store for us."

Alex smiled wide. He loved that his man 'got' him. While he realised his way of doing things was a little eccentric, he couldn't hide that some of the most enjoyable experiences of his life had been rooted in his imagination. Well, at least until he met Nick. Now he want to share his imagination and crazy ideas with someone who truly understood why they were important to Alex. He was so blessed to have found a kind, caring and beautiful man like Nick.

"Finish your dinner. I have to show you the rest of the resort."

Nick looked genuinely excited. Like a kid on Christmas morning. How appropriate.

Chapter 8

NICK cleaned his plate in record time, excited to see what else his boy had in store for him. He had been shocked to hear the lengths Alex had gone to to stave off cabin fever before he met him, but couldn't help but love how his boy always seemed to come up with unique solutions to his problems.

While he had been initially saddened to realise this little fantasy had been inspired by Alex's past life of reclusive loneliness, his boy's imaginative spark and infectious enthusiasm was easy to get swept up in. The idea of turning your house into a holiday destination was quirky, but since Nick didn't have many good memories of Christmas, and hadn't really celebrated the holiday in years, Alex's exotic alternative was a refreshing change of pace. Besides, if it meant they could explore more stuff like their recent experience in the pool, a bit of quirkiness couldn't be all that bad.

When Alex had first moved in with Nick, it took some time for his boy to adapt to living not only with another person, but in the outside world in general. He found it difficult to be around other people, and wasn't keen on going out on his own. Nick had carefully suggested that Alex might benefit from speaking with a therapist. His boy had initially resisted, claiming 'therapy was for crazy people.' But once Nick had explained that he himself had spoken with a therapist from time to time to discuss his own personal issues, Alex had been more receptive. Alex eventually agreed to try therapy, and it didn't take him long to develop new coping skills and open up to his therapist about his experiences living in prolonged isolation, and the fear that motivated him to hide away from the world.

Alex interrupted his woolgathering by ordering Nick upstairs to have a shower.

"Join me," he said to his boy, purposefully making his voice husky and seductive. A shower together where he could explore his boy's body and make him shudder with desire sounded like a good idea to him.

"I can't. I have to go set some things up. Go and shower. When you're done, meet me in the Relaxation Suite," Alex said with a coy smile.

Relaxation Suite? What the hell is he talking about?

"Don't worry, you'll figure it out."

Nick shook his head with a confused smile, then headed up the stairs as ordered. He showered quickly, then towel-dried himself roughly before slipping into his fluffy robe which was hanging on the hook behind the bathroom door.

As Nick stepped out of the master bedroom and into the upstairs hallway, he heard soft acoustic guitar music coming from one of the spare bedrooms. He also detected the heady scents of jasmine and sandalwood in the air. He followed his nose down the hall to the spare room, and found Alex dressed in a tight white t-shirt and a pair of very short, black workout shorts. Nick's mouth went dry.

The room was dark, lit only by a few scented candles. Alex was standing next to the big folding massage table that was usually downstairs in the workout room. The soft guitar music was coming from Alex's phone that was sitting on the speaker dock, which had apparently been brought up from the kitchen. Another potted palm tree stood in the corner of the room, complete with tinsel decorating the fronds and a pineapple at it's base.

Alex had someone managed to create an amazing spa treatment room for them. Nick was stunned. His boy was a genius, and had seemingly thought of everything. He had even brought up one of the small side tables from the living room to hold various massage oils and the speaker dock.

"Ah, Good Evening Sir. You're right on time for your full body massage appointment. Here is your towel, if you would like to disrobe. Once you are comfortable on the table, we can begin."

Nick's cock was hard in seconds. Alex's outfit was sensational. Plus, the idea of a full body massage from his boy sounded like heaven.

Work had been leaving Nick super stressed lately, and he knew Alex had been trying to find ways to help him unwind and relax. A long, sensual massage from his boy would fit the bill nicely, and he couldn't wait to return the favour. Any excuse to explore Alex's round, sensuous body.

Alex turned himself toward the table with the massage oils while Nick quickly took of his robe, placed it on a chair in the corner, and situated himself, face down, on the padded massage table. He draped the towel over his backside, although he didn't quite understand why Alex wanted him to do that. Was this another role playing game? Nick couldn't wait to find out.

Alex turned around and closed the bedroom door, cutting off the hallway light. The room was now bathed in a warm, orange glow from the scented candles. The heady scents, the candles and the soft music were instantly relaxing. Nick felt some of his tension melt away, and Alex hadn't even started the massage. Alex drizzled some warming massage oil over Nick's back, then began smoothing it across the wide, muscular planes of his shoulders.

"Have you enjoyed your stay at the resort so far, Sir?"

Nick smiled and let his eyes slip closed.

"Yes. The staff have been most accommodating to my needs."

"Well, we do love to ensure our guests get the service they deserve," Alex whispered seductively.

"Oh, I do hope so. Servicing is just what I need."

"Then you just lie there and relax, Sir. Let me do what I do. I guarantee, you've never had a massage like this before."

Nick could feel his cock getting harder by the second. Alex had been so shy and unsure of himself when they first met. But over the last year, he had really come out of his shell. Nick was so happy to not only see his boy happy, but open to expressing his sexuality and desires without feeling ashamed or worried about being judged.

Alex set to work massaging Nick's neck, shoulders, back, arms and legs until every muscle and tendon was loose and free of even the slightest hint of stress. Months of tension melted away like ice cream and Nick was so consumed by his boy's magical touch, he could barely think. He just lay there and moaned as Alex put his heart and soul into what was probably the best massage of his life.

Alex then removed the towel, exposing Nick's buttocks. Nick had expected him to massage them too, but was surprised when Alex started kissing his way up the back of his legs. His hot lips leaving fire in their wake. He then carefully adjusted Nick's legs so they dangled either side of the massage table, his feet resting gently on the carpeted floor.

What is he doing?

Nick suddenly felt a little exposed. He was used to being the dominant partner in the bedroom, but loved it when they switched things up from time to time and had Alex call the shots.

"You said you wanted to be serviced, Sir. I hope this fulfils your request."

Alex carefully spread Nick's muscled globes and pressed his face between them, his hot tongue teasing and caressing Nick's sensitive pucker. It was like lightening travelling through his body straight to his cock. They had never done this before. While Nick loved to rim Alex, he'd never really though about having his boy return the favour. In fact, Nick had never experienced this before with anyone. Perhaps it was his own inhibitions that had held him back, or perhaps his own stereotypes about what a top should and shouldn't do, but whatever the reason, he had always felt this was something he should do for his partner – not the other way around.

The sensitive nerve clusters around his hole where alive with deep, energetic sensations he had never even dreamed of before now. When

Alex's tongue eventually breached his outer ring, Nick thought his head was going to explode.

Why have I never tried this before?!?

It was incredible. Nick couldn't contain his moans of ecstasy as his boy teased and pleasured him with his amazing tongue, and used his hands to gently massage the plain of skin behind his balls.

"If you keep doing that, I'm going to come."

"Then turn over, Sir, and I'll continue servicing you."

Nick flipped over on the massage table and his throbbing cock was finally free. Nick watched as Alex, with lustful fire in his eyes, slowly moved forward and took Nick's cock in his willing mouth. Nick lay back as his boy carefully suckled at the crown before gently working his way down, taking more and more until his nose was buried in the little bush of hair at the base of Nick's shaft. Nick's eyes crossed and his boy relaxed his throat muscles and took ever inch of him with practiced ease. He looked down to see Alex looking back at him, his eyes wide and alive with pleasure. His boy always loved getting throat fucked.

Nick grabbed Alex's head with both hands, gripping his hair firmly.

"I'm so close. Are you ready?" he panted, trying to maintain his control.

Alex nodded, and did his best to smile with a mouthful of cock. Nick began thrusting in and out of his boy's throat. Slow at first, then picking up the pace as he felt his orgasm building. When Alex moaned around his cock, the vibration went straight to his balls. He felt them draw up and within moments, Nick was roaring as his orgasm ripped through him. He felt his cock pulsing deep inside Alex, shooting hot come into his boy's waiting throat. He hadn't come this hard in years, and when his orgasm slowly subsided, Nick felt boneless and light-headed as he released Alex's head and felt him swallowing over and over until his cock with limp.

Alex was right. He'd never had a massage quite like it.

Chapter 9

AFTER ALEX finished giving his man his special massage, he was quickly the recipient of an equally mind-blowing massage from Nick, leaving him boneless, relaxed and physically drained from an orgasm that had him flying.

Nick lifted him into his strong, muscular arms and carried him to bed as if Alex weighed nothing at all. Alex recalled the first time Nick had done this, how he had been terrified Nick would drop him. As strong and powerful as Nick was, he wasn't all that confident that even Nick, the muscle-bound man-mountain with the physique of a god, could handle carrying his bulk. But Alex needn't have worried. Nick chuckled as he effortlessly picked him up and enjoyed the look of shock on Alex's face. This time though, Nick simply smiled, kissed him on the forehead and carefully carried him to their bedroom, gently lowering him onto the bed.

When morning broke, it was Christmas Eve and Alex slowly opened his eyes, enjoying the warmth of the early morning sun. Nick was fast asleep, softly snoring, face down beside him. Alex enjoyed the moment of tranquility before carefully getting up without disturbing his slumbering lover. He quietly moved to the bathroom and went through his normal morning routine.

Once showered and dressed, Alex went downstairs to the kitchen to begin prepping breakfast. He started by cutting up two of the many pineapples that currently inhabited their home, loading the freshly cut fruit into the large blender on the kitchen counter. Alex switched on the appliance, and within seconds the fruit was liquified. He had recently purchased the blender online after reading favourable reviews about it's whisper-quiet operation. Since Nick enjoyed making early morning smoothies, a quiet blender was a godsend. Alex smiled as he watched the pineapple being blended in almost total silence. He jokingly hoped the blender could teach it's bench mate, the devil coffee machine, it's silent secrets.

Alex strained the pineapple slurry into a jug, then reloaded the blender with more fruit including oranges, apples and a couple of bananas. He repeated the process, then added the strained and blended fruit into the jug and gave it a good stir. A quick taste told him the juice was perfect, and he set the jug aside in the fridge to chill.

Next, he set about making some omelettes with bacon, spinach and a little cheese. Alex knew the smell of cooking food was guaranteed to awaken his man. Sure enough, a few minutes later Nick groggily stepped into the kitchen, wound his arms around Alex from behind and began kissing, licking and sucking his neck. Alex moaned and giggled as Nick alternated between one spot that tickled and that one spot that made his eyes roll into the back of his head.

"Merry Christmas Eve, sleepyhead," Alex said when Nick was finished suckling what would no doubt be an enormous hickey onto his neck. He turned and saw Nick admiring his handiwork, a cocky smile on his lips.

"Merry Christmas Eve to you too, babe."

Nick leaned in for a quick, chaste kiss, then headed over to the devil coffee machine. Alex had officially given up trying to get into the infernal machine's psychotic good graces, so coffee making was now strictly Nick's domain. He knew Nick thought his 'irrational' dislike for the coffee machine was borderline insane, but Alex was just done with starting every single morning with a frustrating, flustering death match between man and machine. He also suspected Nick secretly enjoyed being the only one able to use the bastard coffee machine seamlessly without the slightest hint of trouble. Or at the very least, enjoyed how much it annoyed Alex that Nick could use it without trouble. More than once, Alex had threatened to replace the machine, but Nick had argued, some might say sensibly, that this machine worked perfectly and it would be a waste. Alex had to reluctantly agree with this argument, but it didn't stop him fantasising about 'accidentally' knocking the coffee machine off the kitchen counter while dusting, and watching it smash into a million pieces on the floor. That would be such a shame. Truly a tragedy. Alex smiled evilly to himself and tried not to cackle like a witch.

"So, what's on the agenda today?" Nick asked, breaking Alex demented train of thought.

"No agenda. We're in Hawaii. Our only agenda is to relax and enjoy ourselves."

"Okay, let me rephrase. What are our plans for today?"

"Well, I thought a visit to the tropical lagoon, then maybe we could go to the beach and make sandcastles," Alex said grinning.

Nick looked confused. "We're leaving the house."

"No..." Alex said cryptically, now smirking. He plated up the omelettes and brought them over to the kitchen table along with the chilled jug of juice. Nick was clearly still a little confused, but just shrugged and brought their coffees over.

Once breakfast was finished and the dishes washed, dried and put away, Alex lead Nick out onto the entertaining deck, then on to the pool area. He was very happy with how his 'tropical lagoon' had turned out. The potted palms and the giant Tiki statue really set the mood and made it feel like they were actually in Hawaii. He was thankful the potted palms were just rentals, and they would all be taken away in a few days. As much as he liked them, even he had to admit he had gone a bit overboard with them, and having them in and around the house all year round would quickly become difficult to manage.

The two men relaxed and enjoyed swimming in the crisp cool water for a couple of hours, the morning sun warm but not too hot. Nick's skin was already turning that beautiful shade of brown it always did when he spent time in the sun, his tan accentuating his ripped muscular body. Alex could just sit and stare at him, ripped with only a skimpy pair of swim shorts to cover his modesty, all day long.

"What are you staring at?" Nick said playfully.

"Just admiring the view."

"Oh, yeah?" Nick grinned wolfishly, then began hamming it up bydoing his body building poses, showing off his amazing body. He put on an amazing show and started laughing when Alex virtually started drooling at the display.

"So, how about a sandcastle competition?" Alex suggested with s cheeky smile.

"Competition?" That had Nick's attention. He was very competitive in just about everything he did, "What's the prize?"

"Gentleman's choice."

Nick's eyes glittered, and his lips formed into a cocky smirk. Alex knew what that look meant. He was in for an interesting afternoon. He stood up from his deck chair, grabbed two small plastic buckets from behind the chair and passed one to Nick.

"Here, fill this with pool water, then follow me to our private beach," Alex left Nick looking slightly confused and headed out of the fenced off pool area.

Between the pool and the entertaining deck was a small strip of garden. At one end of the carefully maintained lawn was a small flowerbed. The other end was a tool shed and washing line. Alex headed toward the garden bed end and carefully sat down in front of a large inflatable children's pool. It was currently covered in a large, blue, plastic tarpaulin. When Nick joined him he looked around skeptically.

"So, where's our private beach?"

Alex grinned, then carefully removed the tarpaulin, revealing the paddling pool filled with crisp, white sand. Alex's assistant had hated him for suggesting this, mainly because Kelly was the one who would have to be stuck with the task of dragging six heavy sacks of sand from the car. But the end result was amazing. Nick looked at the 'private beach' in stunned silence for a moment before bursting out laughing.

"You really thought of everything, didn't you?"

"What's a trip to Hawaii without a visit to the world famous Waikiki Beach?"

Nick smiled broadly and shook his head. Alex was aware a children's paddling pool filled with sand was far from being an acceptable analogue for Waikiki Beach, but it was the thought that counts.

Alex told Nick to carefully pour the water over the sand so they could begin building their sandcastles. Damp sand was always best for building sturdy sandcastles. They then each took a plastic bucket and started filling them with the now moistened sand.

Alex watched as Nick, smiling like a little boy, began creating the sandcastle to end all sandcastles. His heart expanded at how something so simple could bring his man such joy. If Alex had had any doubts about his crazy holiday plan, just seeing Nick relax and enjoy himself like this was all the proof he needed to sweep those doubts away.

Nick wasn't the only one enjoying their trip to the beach. Alex was enjoying mucking about in the sand too. Unlike Nick, Alex had never actually been to a beach before. Although he had many opportunities to visit one of Melbourne's pristine beaches since he moved in with Nick, he hadn't yet felt comfortable enough to do it. Too many people. Too many judgemental eyes watching him. Although Alex felt better about his body and appearance since meeting Nick, he was still very self-conscious about baring his body and scars in public.

"I just thought, how do we determine the winner?" Nick asked, his competitive steak showing.

"How about we both win, that way we both get a prize?"

"Hmmm, sounds interesting. I like it. Especially if it means I get the prize I'm thinking of. I'm looking forward to it." Nick said suggestively, waggling his eyebrows.

"And I'm looking forward to getting mine," Alex said equally suggestively. He smiled and couldn't believe a little innuendo between them could be enough to get him hard already.

They spent the next hour creating magnificent sculptures in the sand. Well, the were sculptures at the very least. Their magnificence was very much open to debate. Alex's castle looked like it was melting, and Nick's was top heavy and had serious structural issues. When Nick's castle suddenly collapsed, taking Alex's crumbling sand shack with it, they both agreed that they should stick to their day jobs. Building design was clearly not in their wheelhouses.

"So, since mine kinda destroyed yours, I guess that means you technically won first. Name your prize!" Nick said, waggling his eyebrows again.

Alex made a point of pondering his options dramatically, making lots of exaggerated "hmmm" sounds. Eventually he smiled coyly and looked deep into his man's eyes.

"Okay, lets go inside."

Chapter 10

NICK HAD no idea what Alex was about to suggest, but he was up for anything. His boy looked very nervous, but also excited. Nick had learned early on in their relationship that Alex was very shy when it came to expressing his needs in the bedroom. Yet, over the last few months, he had gained a little more confidence, and was now willing to speak up when he was keen to try something new, but Nick noticed his boy still needed to 'psych' himself up first.

Alex led Nick upstairs to their bedroom and proceeded into the bathroom. He began stripping off his clothes and Nick followed suit.

A sexy shower? Is that all? Well, if it makes my boy happy...

Nick had been expecting something a little more... exotic. Since they have fun in the shower all the time, he was a little surprised that this would be Alex's chosen prize.

"Between the pool and the sand, we need to clean up before we get into it." Alex said, smirking every so slightly. He wasn't giving anything away.

So, not a sexy shower. Cheeky boy. What have you got planned?

They both stepped into the double sized shower cubical and promptly began rinsing away the sand and chlorine. It didn't take long for Nick to realise that Alex was maintaining as much distance as possible, and was also clearly trying to avoid touching Nick. Normally, Alex was very tactile when they shared the shower.

Nick added a little body wash to the shower puff and began gently soaping up Alex's back, but his boy immediately froze.

"No, don't. Not yet."

"Is everything okay, Alex? Are you in pain?"

Nick understood Alex suffered from severe back pain and nerve problems related to the injuries he sustained when Alex was the victim of a frenzied stabbing attack many years ago. Even after the best part of a decade, Alex continued to suffer from periodic back pain and loss of mobility. Thankfully, Nick had managed to convince Alex to visit some specialists to get his conditions reassessed, since he hadn't been seeing doctors regularly while he had lived alone in his little isolated house.

Over the last year, a combination of regular physiotherapy, a light exercise routine with one of Nick's highly qualified personal trainers, plus an adjustment to his medications had seen a slight improvement to his boy's pain management. But ultimately, nothing would ever be able to undo the damage inflicted by Adrian Jackson. There would still be days when Alex would be in severe pain, and days where he would be unable to walk more than a few steps without assistance. Nick was committed to supporting Alex no matter what, and would do anything to ensure his boy was as healthy and pain-free as humanly possible.

"No, I'm fine. It's nothing like that. I just don't want you to touch me."

Nick was aghast. Something was terribly wrong.

Alex doesn't want me to touch him? What was going on?

Nick tried to remember if Alex had been angry or upset at any point today, but couldn't think of anything. Everything had been fine up until the sand castle building. Was Alex angry with him for knocking over his sandcastle?

"Relax, I can see you freaking out. I'm not angry with you. I just... have a fantasy, and I need your help with it. It'll make sense in a minute, I promise."

While Nick felt a wave of relief sweep over him, he was simultaneously hit with a tsunami of confusion. Alex's fantasy was to not be touched by Nick. Did that mean he didn't like being touched? Nick was completely lost.

The two men jumped out of the shower and briskly towelled themselves dry. They returned to the bedroom, not bothering to get dressed. Alex went over to the bedside table and pulled something out, then sat down on the edge of the bed.

"What have you got planned? You're being so mysterious."

Alex smiled and held up two long black silk scarves. Nick had never seen them before and presumed they must be new. What were they for?

"Okay, you've got my attention. What's your fantasy?"

"Promise you won't think I'm weird?" Alex was blushing deep red. Nick tried to hide his amusement. Whatever the fantasy was, Alex was really turned on by it, and even a little embarrassed.

This is going to be fun!

"I would never think you're weird, babe. I've always said we are both able to discuss our wants and needs without embarrassment or judgement. But, I must admit... I'm very intrigued." Nick took a slow step toward Alex.

"Okay, I want to lie down on the bed, have you blindfold me, then tie my hands above my head."

Whoa! Not what I was expecting at all.

Nick and Alex hadn't done much in the way of bondage or restraints. Who knew Alex had this kink? Nick's cock, which was already hard, was starting to throb. He took another step forward.

"Then what?" Nick said, almost dry mouthed.

"Then... I want you to talk dirty to me."

Nick smiled wolfishly, and took another step closer, now standing right in front of his boy.

"And then?"

"Well, I don't want you to touch me at all. I want..." Alex blushed again.

"Yes?"

"I... want to see if you can make me come, just by using your voice." he said quietly, his head bowed, not able to make eye contact.

"Wow. That sounds... I've never done anything like that before. It sounds hot as fuck though."

"Really?" Alex looked straight up at Nick, with hope in his eyes.

"Really. Let's do it!"

Nick was super excited. Alex always said he loved his voice, especially in bed, but he had no idea his voice had that much affect of his boy! He had no idea if he could actually do what Alex wanted, but he was willing to give it his best damn shot. If nothing, seeing Alex trussed up and at his mercy would be seriously hot. He couldn't wait to begin.

"I love you, Alex."

"I love you too, Nick."

Chapter 11

ALEX WAS shaking with nervous excitement. From virtually the first time they met, Alex had been strangely aroused by Nick's voice. He remembered the day they met. He was soaked head to toe in iced coffee. Nick followed him into the lift of that office building. When Nick leaned in from behind, close to his ear, and spoke quietly but with that low, sexy voice of his, it made Alex shake all over. It was instant and inexplicable. It made every nerve in his body light up like a Christmas tree. He'd never felt anything like it before.

Ever since, whenever Nick spoke to him in *that voice*, Alex had the same visceral reaction. It was primal. It was deep. It was hot as fuck. Which got Alex to thinking: could Nick get him off just by talking? No touching. No sex. Just his voice and his filthy mind.

Alex had been keen to find out for ages if it were possible, but had always been a little afraid that Nick would think his little fantasy was silly. He shouldn't have worried. He should have realised that Nick would never make fun of him for expressing his desires. But right now, he was kicking himself for not bringing up the subject a whole lot sooner, since Nick appeared to be just as excited about experimenting with this fantasy as he was.

Alex stood up and handed Nick the two black silk scarves, then turned away. Nick took one of the scarves and carefully placed it over Alex's eyes, ensuring he couldn't see anything, then tied the blindfold with simple bow. He then allowed Nick to guide him to the bed, where he lay down, face up and placed his hands above his head, waiting for Nick to tie them up with the other scarf.

"I'm going to tie your hands loosely, so you'll be able to release yourself at anytime if you need to." Nick said as he secured Alex's hands to the one of the banisters on the iron bed head. He gently draped a strand of the scarf in one of his hands.

"Just pull on this, and the knot with come undone, but just in case it doesn't, you're safe word is 'red'. You say it, and everything stops and I'll untie you immediately. Do you understand?"

"Yes, Sir." Alex's breath hitched as he heard Nick's soft growl of approval, his man clearly pleased at his use of the honorific.

Alex couldn't see anything and couldn't really move. He was completely at Nick's mercy. It was exciting. He wasn't sure how he would feel about being restrained like this, but he trusted Nick with his life. He knew Nick wanted to explore kinkier stuff in the bedroom, but Alex had always been a little intimidated by mainstream BDSM. He wasn't into the whole whips and chains thing; and if he was into pain, he didn't need to be beaten to a bloody pulp with a cat o'nine tails to get it. He could just bring the groceries into the house unassisted.

Today was about Alex's fantasies. But he wanted Nick to enjoy it too. So he wanted to experiment with mild BDSM beyond simple domination. So far, he was enjoying being restrained. He felt the bed dip slightly, and could feel Nick stretching out beside him.

Although he couldn't see anything, he could feel his other senses working overtime to compensate. He could hear Nick breathing. He could smell his sharp, masculine scent. He could feel the way the mattress dipped slightly as Nick shifted his body to get comfortable. Although Nick wasn't touching him, he was close enough that Alex could feel his body heat radiating off of his bare skin. Alex suspected Nick was laying on his side, but couldn't be certain.

"Look at you, boy." Nick's rumbling voice was low and deep, thick with lust and passion, "All trussed up for me and no escaping. You're mine, boy. To do with as I please."

Alex's heart started pumping faster and he felt every hair on his skin stand on end. How was Nick able to provoke this response with just a few short words? The power of his voice was amazing. Alex stifled a moan.

"Would you like to hear all the wicked things I'm going to do to you?"

Alex panted in reply. He could feel his body temperature rising and with each word uttered from Nick's beautiful lips, Alex's body began to slowly writhe and move, as if he was losing his ability to remain still.

"Answer me, boy!" Nick said sharply.

"Yes, Sir! I want to hear what you're going to do."

He could almost hear Nick's smug, wolfish grin. He was clearly enjoying this as much as Alex was.

"First, I'm gonna get you off just by talking to you. Then I'm going to keep your hands tied above your head. I'm going to take my time as I slowly explore every inch of your body with my tongue. Lick you all over, bite you in all those sensitive spots that you love. Make you crazy as I blow your mind. Would you like that, boy?"

Alex was vibrating all over now. "Oh, yes, Sir."

"That's what I thought. You love being mine. You love it when I'm in charge. You love being tied up and at my mercy. Next, I'm going to flip you over so I can explore that glorious round ass of yours. I'm going to lick it, and kiss it, and bite it and, if you're a good boy…" Alex was panting as Nick paused for a moment. He felt Nick shift slightly on the bed, "… I'll spank you until you scream my name." he said in Alex's ear, his hot breath tickling his skin.

"Oh my god!" Alex shouted. His cock had never been this hard. He could feel his precum dribbling down his shaft. He could barely keep still, his body desperate for release.

"My sweet, dirty boy. You like the idea of being spanked. I think you need a firm hand, and I promise to give it to you. I bet I can make you come just from a good, hard spanking. Would you like that? Would you like me to spank you until your balls ache and you see stars?"

"Fuck, yes!" Alex was feeling wild. He couldn't believe how aroused he was. He hadn't even touched himself and, more importantly, neither had Nick. Just his voice and his dirty talk was enough to get him this wound up. It was incredible. This was the most erotic moment of his life so far.

"Once that backside of yours is nice and warmed up, I'll ram my thick cock in to you, and fuck you 'til you scream. You'll be shouting my name and begging to come again. You're mine, boy. Don't ever forget it. I'm going to fuck you so hard, you won't be able to stand afterwards. I'll make you my sex slave and keep you here. You'll just lie here and get fucked over and over. Servicing my cock. Getting that tight throat of yours good and stretched. Would you like that, boy?"

"Nick!" Alex couldn't hold back any more. His body arched and without even the slightest touch, Alex's balls drew up and he came over and over, as thick streams of his hot release coated his belly and chest. He was so wrung out, his breathing ragged. The blind fold was suddenly removed and his wrist binding released. Nick grabbed hold of him and kissed him deeply as he carefully rubbed and massaged his arms and wrists, ensuring his circulation was fine.

"That was the most incredible thing I have ever seen in my life. That was so fucking hot. I'm barely holding back here, babe. I need to come so bad."

Alex smiled widely, his face sweaty and flushed.

"Don't hold back, give it all to me. Anywhere you want."

"I want to come all over your face."

Alex lay back down with a grin, and Nick carefully straddled his chest. Nick's cock looked like it was made of solid granite. He barely touched himself and he was balancing on the edge. Alex leaned his head forward ever so slightly and gently licked the underside of Nick's crown. Nick roared as the light touch of Alex's tongue pushed him over into his thundering orgasm, shooting load after load of hot white come across Alex's face and lips. Nick was shaking all over, the full force of his release sapping him of all energy. He carefully shifted over to his side of the bed and collapsed next to Alex, desperately trying to catch his breath.

Alex just smiled and relaxed. He never thought a simple sandcastle competition could be this exciting.

Chapter 12

AFTER A quick nap and a leisurely lunch, Nick claimed his "prize" from the sandcastle competition. Nick and Alex spent a few hours making slow, passionate love to each other. Once the sun had dipped below the tree line, the two men enjoyed another relaxing dip in the pool.

By mid afternoon, Alex was in the mood for some baking, and decided to whip up some of his Christmas cupcakes for them to enjoy after dinner. Nick enjoyed cooking, but had never mastered the art of baking – despite many valiant attempts by his boy to teach him the ways of the cupcake. Nick preferred to just watch Alex as he created his glorious works of edible art.

Nick watched closely as Alex started to make his famous Christmas Spice cupcakes; a variation on the classic Red Velvet cupcakes, but featuring cinnamon, nutmeg and something called 'allspice'. Nick didn't know what 'allspice' was, but judging by the illicit fingerful of batter he tasted before getting his hand slapped with a spatula, it made the cupcakes taste almost like a traditional Christmas pudding. Once the cupcakes were baked and cooled, Nick was mesmerised as he watched his boy carefully decorate each cupcake with a swirl of rich cream cheese frosting, then adorn each one with a miniature red and white striped candy cane. The end result looked like something out of a patisserie, rather than an everyday suburban kitchen. But Nick would expect nothing less from his Cupcake Boy.

Nick adored the lightly spiced cupcake scent that now floated throughout their home. Leave it to Alex to pick the perfect recipe for creating the perfect ambiance for Christmas Eve. He never thought this house could actually 'smell' like Christmas – but somehow Alex had done it. Alex packed up the cupcakes into a special container, sealed the airtight lid and left them on the kitchen counter. Nick attempted to snatch one of the baked treats for himself, but was quickly informed that they were for after dinner.

"So, what do we have planned for Christmas Eve?" Nick asked as Alex resealed the airtight lid on the cupcake container, his cupcake snatching plan foiled.

"Well, since we had an active day of swimming in the lagoon, walking on Waikiki Beach, sandcastle building and... um... other activities..." Alex blushed deeply, "I thought tonight we would relax and have a Movie Night downstairs?"

Nick loved the idea. A night on the couch with his boy. Sounded perfect to him.

"Excellent. Lead the way!"

Alex lead Nick upstairs where they got changed into comfortable, daggy clothes. Alex threw on a pair of old shorts and a t-shirt. Nick stripped down to nothing, then pulled on a pair of threadbare track pants. The old tracky-dacks were ancient. Worn so thin that they were no longer suitable for keeping him warm in Winter, but they sure were comfortable for lazing around the house watching movies. Plus, he knew from experience that if he wore them with no underwear or shirt, Alex would have a hard time keeping his eyes on the movie. Nick smirked at the thought. He loved flustering his boy.

"Really? Your dodgy sex pants? You haven't had enough today?" Alex tried to sound reproachful, but Nick didn't miss the heat in his boy's eyes.

"I could never have enough of you. Besides, you love my dodgy sex pants!"

"They have more holes than fabric."

"Great for easy access!" Nick said with a broad smile and pumped his hips in the air in an exaggerated display of lewdness. Alex blushed, which only made Nick smile wider.

"Come on, let's get downstairs and kick off our Movie Night." Nick held out his hand to Alex, and the two men walked downstairs until they reached the basement media room.

Nick was stunned by what he saw. Once again, another radical transformation had taken place. The neat, almost minimalist media room had been replaced by another Hawaiian explosion. More decorated potted palm trees, more plastic flower garlands, more tinsel and – surprise surprise – more fruit.

"Seriously? More pineapples? I swear they're multiplying!" Nick said as he counted at least twenty pineapples. Each decorated with different strands of tinsel and festive sunglasses.

"Well, that's pineapples for you. You leave them alone and they start breeding like rabbits." Alex said with a straight face, but then lost it and burst into a fit of giggles.

"They were probably inspired by us, baby."

"Voyeuristic pineapples? I'm not sure I approve of that."

"We'll punish them later for their misdeeds." Nick said in his Big Bad Dom voice, trying to look as stern and intimidating as possible. Alex just giggled joyfully.

"So, what have you got planned for us for dinner?"

"Well, I know it's cheating a little; but while you were in the shower earlier I ordered dinner in. It'll be here soon."

"What did you order?" Nick was intrigued.

"It's a surprise," the doorbell rang. "And there it is. You wait right here, and I'll bring it down. Back in a minute."

Alex made his way up the stairs and headed off to meet the delivery driver. Nick looked around the room, marvelling at the lunatic decorations. He noticed the drinks fridge had been filled with bottles of soft drink. Passiona and fizzy pineapple drink. How very fitting for a tropical theme.

Moments later, Alex returned with two large pizza boxes. Nick shook his head and smiled. Pizza was an interesting choice, both for a tropical theme and Christmas Eve. But Nick noticed the smirk on Alex's face and knew he had something up his sleeve.

When Nick opened the first pizza box, he finally realised why Alex had been smirking. Nick burst out laughing.

"Hawaiian Pizza?" Nick chortled. His boy was deranged. "You know, Hawaiian Pizza isn't actually Hawaiian. It was invented in Canada, apparently."

"Shut up! It's a very ancient, very traditional dish enjoyed by all..."

"Canadians!"

Alex couldn't hold back his laughter and surrendered to the hilarity of the situation.

"I also ordered a Meatlovers pizza, so technically this is a Luau.'

"You've lost your mind!"

"Yeah, but you still love me."

Nick put the pizza boxes down on the coffee table and kissed his boy deeply.

"Yeah, I do. Merry Christmas Eve, Alex"

"Merry Christmas Eve, Nick."

The two men sat down on their newly acquired leather reclining sofa. The two matching recliner arm chairs were still there, but Nick loved snuggling up with his boy while they watched movies, so he had found a matching couch that had similar reclining and massage functions. The result was possibly the most comfortable, yet pricey piece of furniture Nick had ever bought. Alex had nearly hit the roof when he found out how much it cost, but no price was too high if it meant they could comfortably snuggle together during their regular movie marathons.

"What are we watching?" Nick asked as Alex used his phone to open the app that controlled all the home theatre equipment.

"Something fun and theme appropriate."

The lights dimmed slowly until they went out. The massive wall-sized screen switched on and the movie began.

Blue Hawaii starring Elvis Presley.

Nick couldn't wipe the smile off his face. It was the perfect choice. Alex was a genius.

After Blue Hawaii was finished, they switched to a more traditional Christmas film, Miracle on 34th Street, followed by Home Alone 2: Lost in New York. Nick loved the last movie. It had been one of his favourites when he was a kid. It was a silly movie, but the perfect way to round off their Christmas movie marathon.

It was getting late, and after a long and eventful day, the two men were officially wiped out. They quickly gathered up the empty pizza boxes, threw them in the rubbish, then made their way upstairs to bed.

Chapter 13

CHRISTMAS MORNING was slow and lazy. Alex and Nick slept in until just after ten. When they both woke up, they started the day by making love, then taking a long, luxurious shower together.

Once they were dressed; Nick in his board shorts and plastic lei, Alex in a bright red Hawaiian shirt and green shorts; the two men went downstairs to the kitchen to rustle up some breakfast. Alex set to work making a bacon and egg frittata with spinach and red capsicum, while Nick wrangled the devil coffee machine, made a fruit salad and finally some toast. Soon they were sat at the kitchen table enjoying their Christmas morning breakfast feast.

The old cuckoo clock that hung on the wall chimed as they started to eat, and Alex silently wished Darla a Merry Christmas. Whenever he heard the old clock chime, he felt that her spirit was in the room, watching over him.

Nick clearly enjoyed the frittata, evidenced by his appreciative moans which had Alex's toes curling. Alex loved the fruit salad that Nick had made. For a man who once hated fruit salad, Nick had become inspired by Alex's slightly non-traditional recipe and had started making all sorts of glorious variations.

As they polished off their breakfast, and everything appeared to be fine and relaxed, Alex couldn't help but notice that Nick appeared to be a little distracted. He seemed tense, like he was worried about something.

"Is everything okay?"

Nick took a second to respond, as if he hadn't heard Alex speak, but then snapped out of it, eventually smiling. "Oh yes, everything's just fine, babe. Merry Christmas!" he said as he held up his glass of orange juice. They clinked glasses.

"Speaking of Christmas, if you've finished you're breakfast, follow me out to the living room."

Alex rose from his seat, placed his plate and cutlery in the dishwasher then wandered out to the living room, with Nick trailing close behind.

Alex reached down beneath the largest of the decorated palm trees and retrieved Nick's Christmas gift. He had wrapped it in fine gold paper and a delicate white ribbon only minutes before Nick got home from his office meeting the other day. He'd managed to hide it under the sofa only seconds before Nick had got inside, then discreetly placed it under the tree last night as they were heading up to bed.

"Oh, baby, you didn't have to get me anything."

"I know, but I wanted to. I hope you like it." Alex handed Nick the carefully wrapped gift.

"Can I open it now?"

"Of course! It's Christmas after all!"

Nick started slowly and carefully untying the ribbon, then ever so slowly trying to unwrap the paper-covered box.

"Oh, just rip it off!" Alex was getting impatient, he wanted to see if Nick liked the gift. Nick smirked, then dutifully ripped the gold paper off and opened the box, revealing a dark navy blue t-shirt.

"A t-shirt? Wow, thanks baby."

"Take it out! Take it out!"

Nick gingerly removed the garment from the box, unfolded it and held it up. Printed on the front of the shirt in big, bold letters were the words "I'M THE BOSS OF YOU!"

Nick laughed out loud and smiled from ear to ear at his gift.

He likes it! He actually likes it! YES!

"Thank you, baby! This is amazing. I love it!" He proceeded to put the t-shirt on, discovering quickly that it was very form fitting.

"It's a little snug..."

Alex giggled, "Yeah, that was intentional. If you're the boss, you gotta show off those powerful muscles!"

"I think you just like me wearing tight clothes so you can perv on me!"

"I can't deny that." Alex grinned.

Nick kissed Alex and thanked him again for his gift. He then took off the shirt and put it back in it's box, saying he'll save it for after their 'holiday' and wear it when he visits the various gym locations.

"My local managers will get such a kick out of it."

Alex wondered if Nick had gotten him a gift too. Not that he really cared that much. Spending time with the man he loved and having a relaxing Hawaiian trip was more than he'd ever had at Christmas for a very long time.

"I have something for you too," Nick said, his face looking serious. "Close your eyes and wait here."

Alex closed his eyes and heard Nick walk up the stairs. A few moments later, he heard Nick return.

"Can I open my eyes yet?" Alex was excited, and the anticipation was delicious.

"Not yet. Keep them closed until I say." Nick carefully guided Alex to sit down on the couch.

"Well?"

"Okay. Open your eyes."

Alex slowly opened them. Nick was directly in front of him, down on one knee.

"Alex Michaels, you are the most extraordinary man I have ever met. You are kind, pure, generous, funny and above all else, loving. I can't imagine my life without you, and I don't even want to try. You've made me so happy, and you are the other half of my soul. So, will you do me the honour of becoming my husband?"

Nick held up a small velvet box, opened it and revealed a simple but elegant ring. Two interlaced bands, one silver and one gold. Alex's vision began to blur as he couldn't hold back his joyful tears.

"Yes! Yes, I will!"

Nick place the ring gently on Alex's finger, then kissed him deeply and passionately. Alex's head swam and he felt like he was going to burst into flames.

"You don't know what this means to me. I can't wait to walk down the aisle with you. I can't wait for you to be mine."

"Me too. I love you so much, Nick. You've changed my life for the better, and not a day goes by that I don't thank God for that day you drenched me in iced coffee."

Nick laughed. "Best accident ever. Merry Christmas, Alex."

"Merry Christmas, husband to be."

THE END

AFTERWORD

I hope you have enjoyed reading "Christmas With The Cupcake Boy" as much as I have enjoyed writing it. It was so much fun to revisit these characters and give them a quick little festive story.

I have a feeling this won't be the last we hear from Alex and Nick, as their voices are still ever present in the back of my mind, crying out for another story. And who am I to deny them? Perhaps one last adventure before they get married? Only time will tell...

In the meantime, I am currently working on Men Of Melbourne #3, which I hope to have out there sometime in the first half of 2020. Stay tuned to my social media and my website for more info as it comes to hand!

A big thank you to all of you out there who have bought my books, left reviews, shared recommendations with your friends and sent me messages of support throughout the year. Your kindness and generosity of spirit are most appreciated.

So Happy Holidays to you all, and I hope you have a wonderful and prosperous New Year. Have a cupcake for me!

Lots of Love

Alex Leslie

Don't miss out!

Visit the website below and you can sign up to receive emails whenever Alex Leslie publishes a new book. There's no charge and no obligation.

https://books2read.com/r/B-A-CCJI-SNACB

BOOKS2READ

Connecting independent readers to independent writers.

About the Author

Alex Leslie is an Australian-born author of Gay M/M romance works including *Chasing The Cupcake Boy, Hearts Unfrozen, Following His Bliss* and *My Big Gay Family Christmas Fiasco.*

Alex lives with his partner, two troublesome cats (who love sleeping on his laptop!) and is currently dealing with an ongoing addiction to iced coffee drinks.

Read more at www.alexleslieauthor.com.